Back Yard Angel

Back Yard Angel

JUDY DELTON

Illustrated by Jill Weber

Houghton Mifflin Company
Boston

Library of Congress Cataloging-in-Publication Data

Delton, Judy.
Back yard Angel.

Summary: Although ten-year-old Angel loves her little
brother Rags dearly, the constant responsibility of taking care
of him weighs heavily on her young shoulders.
[1. Brothers and sisters—Fiction.   2. Baby sitters—Fiction.
3. Responsibility—Fiction]   I. Title.
PZ7.D388Bac   1983   [Fic]   82-23409
ISBN 0-395-96060-6

Printed in the United States of America
HAD 10 9 8 7 6 5 4 3 2 1

For Nancy, gratefully

CONTENTS

ONE

Warm Up with Oil

Angel O'Leary sat on her back steps, frowning. She frowned most of the time. Every week when her mother's friend Alyce stopped by, she would say (as soon as she had climbed the steps past Angel and was inside the door), "Doesn't that child ever smile?"

And every time, her mother would sigh and reply, "No, she always looks so glum, as if she'd lost her best friend."

But Angel hadn't lost her best friend. She didn't have a best friend.

Sometimes when Mrs. O'Leary saw her daughter frowning she would put her arm around Angel and ask gently what was the matter, and sometimes she shook her by the shoulders and asked what was the matter, and finally, when Angel kept frowning, she took her to the doctor and asked *him* what was the matter. He talked to Angel all over again, then told her mother it was just a stage she was going through. He said it was the age for going through stages. Mrs. O'Leary looked relieved, though she had always thought that stages came during the "terrible twos" and maybe again at twelve or thirteen. She had never heard of a stage at ten.

"She's not a happy child," Alyce continued to say every time she stepped around Angel on the back steps, sitting with her chin in her hands.

Angel wasn't particularly unhappy. She just didn't have any reason to smile. Her face seemed to fall naturally into a frown. All the creases pointed down. Someday she would smile. Perhaps when she was older and could travel out of her neighborhood and make friends of her own. Right now she had a good reason to frown most of the time. It was her younger brother, Rags. Angel was in charge of Rags's life. Ever since their father had left them, before Rags was born (Angel didn't remember her father very well), their mother seemed to have one goal in life, and that was to keep her family safe. Since Mrs. O'Leary had a part-time job, keeping Rags safe was Angel's responsibility most of the time.

"Baby-sitting is not just a job, Angel," her mother would say. "It means being responsible for someone's very life."

Rags's life weighed heavily on Angel's shoulders. It seemed monumental.

"Remember, don't cross the street. Don't go off the block with Rags," her mother would warn on her way to work.

Angel remembered. How could she forget? She had hardly been off the block herself except for school. Her whole summer was spent on their one block bounded by Kilbourn Avenue,

Brownell Street, Maple, and Elm, being in charge of Rags's life. In the first grade she had learned about guardian angels and now she decided she was one. Her name was Angel, and she was the guardian of Rags's life.

Actually, Angel's real name was Caroline. Her mother started calling her Angel because she was always in some kind of trouble. In order to sound loving, even though she was feeling very cross, her mother would begin her lectures by saying, "Now, why in the world would you do a thing like that, Angel?" As Mrs. O'Leary said, she may be angry at the things Angel *did,* but she still loved *her.*

Rags was called Rags because when he was little he always carried the remains of an old blanket around with him. His real name was Theodore.

Both children and their mother lived in an old green house with black shutters and an artificial fireplace. In the back yard was a swing set and by the side of the house, next to the back door, was a cement urn filled with petunias.

Along the house grew thick green ferns. In the winter these were covered with snow.

Angel went to St. Mary's school, but now school was out for the summer. She was glad. School was the same as home. She would think she was doing something well, only to have the teacher shake her head and sigh just as Angel's mother did, except that the teacher didn't soften it by calling her Angel. The teacher called her Caroline, which sounded very angry.

Ever since school had closed in late spring, Angel sat on the back steps every morning. When she was younger she had sat waiting to be old enough to go to school. Now she just sat waiting.

Rags came around the corner of the house from the swing set, where he had been playing. His face was dirty and his hair looked as if he had crawled into a small space where there was room enough only for him and not for the unruly thatch that covered the top of his head. He was carrying an old rag instead of his blanket.

"Let's climb up on the oil truck," he said.

5

Angel looked down the block to the gray stone house. Sure enough, the oil truck was parked alongside it, as usual. The man who lived there drove the truck, which was very high and had a small ladder going from the door of the cab up and around to a narrow ledge. From the ledge, anyone could walk all around the tank and see up close the big letters that spelled out WARM UP TO US WITH OIL, and then the smaller letters, *Fast service, free delivery. 302-4489.*

When Angel was little, like Rags, she used to climb up on the truck and pretend she was a mechanic, repairing engines. Sometimes she would pretend she was driving the giant truck. And sometimes she just traced the big red letters with her finger. They were almost as tall as she was. Now Rags liked to climb the metal ladder, too, and pretend things.

Angel rose from the steps and began to stroll toward the gray house with Rags. The oil truck was one of the few things within the boundaries set by her mother. She was never absolutely positive it wasn't forbidden to climb oil trucks, but since no one ever said not to, she supposed it was allowed. Her mother never told her or Rags *not* to climb on oil trucks. And no one around the gray house ever told them not to, either. It wasn't even very exciting anymore, but since Rags enjoyed it, Angel might as well

go along. She wondered if that was the way all of life was: Things were so much fun when you were very small, and then, bang, all of a sudden the excitement was gone. She looked at Rags and suddenly felt sorry for him. Here he was, jumping up and down thinking about the oil truck, and then one day he'd come here and find he didn't want to climb on it anymore. If that's what growing up was, Angel decided, there was no reason to be in a hurry.

When they came to the gray house, Angel looked around. No one seemed to be nearby. Even though they had not been forbidden to go there, she always checked quickly to see if anyone was there who might shout, "Hey, you two get down from there; you could get hurt." Adults were always so worried about children's safety, Angel thought. They always made it sound as though it was for a child's own good when they told you to stop doing something that was fun.

Rags was already starting up the ladder.

"C'mon!" he called. Angel climbed up only as far as the top step and then sat down to look at the neighborhood from this vantage point. She was so used to looking at it from her own steps that she enjoyed the different view this gave. She could see the rest of the back yards, the newly planted gardens. Rags was scampering around the tank playing imaginary games. Angel wished that she was four again. She looked at the wheels of the truck. My! They were *large!* She could probably stand up underneath the truck! She slid down and walked up to the wheels. Not quite. She had to bend to get underneath. Once she was under, it was dark and cozy, like a tree house. "I'll bet no one could find me here!" she said to herself. She hummed a little tune as she went from wheel to wheel investigating the nuts and bolts. "Repairmen should hire me," she thought. "I could reach all these hard places and grease and oil everything." She pretended she was a repairman, oiling nuts and bolts and springs with her imaginary oil can. "Psst, psst, psst," she sang as she oiled. After a long while, she came out from under the truck into the bright daylight and blinked. It had been cool and shady under the truck, but it was getting hot now in the sun. Angel sat on the bottom step of the ladder and frowned. It was quiet all around her. Too quiet. Rags! Where was Rags?

She scampered up the metal ladder, two steps at a time, and raced around the tank of the truck. Rags's life! She was in charge of it, for heaven's sake. "Oh!" she said in relief, when she saw him. "There you are." She was out of breath and sat down on the railing to rest. He was just playing quietly, that's all Rags was doing.

"What's that in your hand, Rags?" Angel could see something red. She stood up and walked quickly over to him. Was Rags bleeding? Oh, she fervently hoped not! All of a sudden, Angel felt a prickly shudder of suspicion. She looked up at the words WARM UP US WITH OIL. The word TO was gone! And Rags was working hard

on the U in US. His tongue was between his teeth, and his little fingers dug under the letter in an attempt to free it.

"*Rags!* Stop that! What are you doing that for?"

"They come *off!*" he said excitedly. "They can all come off!"

Angel took the torn bits of letters Rags had in his hand and tried to piece them back together again. Surely she could put them back. That wouldn't be so hard. She formed the T and put it back where it had been. It fell to the ground. She tried again. It was no use; it wouldn't stick.

"Rags!" she said in alarm. "What are we going to do?"

Rags stood back and looked at the letters that were left. Angel read the words WARM UP US WITH OIL. Everyone would notice that a word was missing. There was only one thing to do. If she took out the word US, it would read, WARM UP WITH OIL, and that made sense, even though there would be a big space in the middle. Angel started peeling off the U and the S. If Rags wondered about her change of mind, he didn't say so. He just helped Angel peel the US off as fast as he could. Even as Angel worked, she felt that familiar sinking in her stomach that meant trouble. Somehow she was involved again in doing something she shouldn't. It seemed ages before the US was removed. When it was, she stepped back and read, "WARM UP WITH OIL." That was clearer anyway. That was the way it should have read in the first place. It was a better slogan. The oil man should thank her. Somehow, Angel didn't think he would.

Picking up the scraps of red, Angel grabbed Rags's hand and helped him climb down from the truck. When they got home, Rags dug a small hole and Angel buried the red letters in the back yard. Then she went to wash her hands. She almost wished a policeman would come to the door, arrest her, and have it over with. As it was, she'd have to wait and wait, wondering if one was around the corner. "This is the way a criminal must feel all the time," she thought, "always worried that the phone or doorbell would ring." Angel kept listening for the phone. It didn't ring. Her mother was humming "Battle Hymn of the Republic" while she defrosted the refrigerator.

Before long Alyce drove up. She looked bright and cheerful in her pink-flowered polyester blouse. "Why in the world is she always so happy?" thought Angel, frowning. Alyce walked around Angel, who was sitting on the back steps again. "Your face is going to grow that way," she sang, patting Angel on the head.

After Alyce was in the house awhile, the phone did ring. Even from outdoors, Angel could feel her mother's muscles tighten, but she couldn't hear what her mother was saying. Just when she thought it was all a mistake and it must be their neighbor Margaret Toomer on the phone, her mother came out on the porch. Alyce was behind her. They both seemed awfully tall to Angel today, looking down at her from the top step.

"Angel?" said her mother lightly. "That was Mrs. Johnson on the phone — from the white house on Brownell Street. She said she saw some children peeling letters off the oil truck down the street this afternoon, and she thought it looked like you and Rags. I told her it couldn't have been. I told her you were here all the time, or just walking around the block."

It was quiet for a long time.

"Weren't you, Angel?" her mother said a little less lightly.

Rags started up the steps. "We peeled the letters off the truck, Mama," he said proudly. Rags

14

never frowned, and he never seemed to know the difference between good and bad, or right and wrong, or what he should say and what he shouldn't. Angel remembered that once, when he was only two, their mother had told him not to eat dirt. He went right out into the back yard and ate a huge mouthful. A moment later, he came to the screen door with mud on his mouth and said, "I ate the dirt. I naughty boy, Mama."

It was one thing to be disobedient, but to run and tell everyone seemed stupid. Even at two.

Now Angel's mother stopped smiling. Alyce was not smiling either. She was frowning and shaking her head from side to side. Her mother looked impatient. Giving her foot a little stamp, she said, "Why would you *do* a thing like that, Angel?"

"Rags took off two letters and then I had to fix it and then we came home."

"We're lucky that Mrs. Johnson didn't call the police."

Angel felt her stomach muscles relax. Her

mother went to call the oil truck man and Mrs. Johnson, and even though Angel's face didn't show it, she smiled inside. It was such a relief to be found out.

Rags was busy digging up the letters Angel had buried. He brought them to her now, covered with dirt, and put them together like a puzzle on the step. TOUS, it said clearly.

It certainly was easy being four, thought Angel. To say what you feel like saying and do the things you feel like doing without worrying about what will happen. She frowned harder than ever at the thought.

TWO

Marie Antoinette

Mrs. O'Leary paid the oil man to have the red letters put back on his truck, and she deducted the cost from Angel's allowance. She talked to Angel and Rags for fifteen minutes about staying near home and out of trouble. For almost a week they played in the yard or in the house.

Today, Angel was pushing Rags on the swing. He seemed not to mind their confinement, but she wished she had some friends of her own. This summer was going to be a long one. None of the girls she knew at school lived in

17

her neighborhood, and of course she couldn't leave her own block. She thought briefly of knocking on the doors of all the houses on the street. Maybe there was a girl her age behind one of those doors. Someone who had just moved in . . .

Angel went to sit on the back steps just as Alyce's car drove up to the curb. "A nickel for a smile," said Alyce, who had to maneuver around Angel to climb the stairs. Angel didn't try to move to one side of the steps; she just stayed where she was, smack dab in the middle. She didn't know why she felt so obstinate, but she did. She didn't feel like moving. They were her steps, after all.

It looked like rain, and Angel was trying to think of what she could do inside the house all day, when it began to thunder. She went inside and up to her room. Her mother called up from the bottom of the stairs to say she was going to the supermarket with Alyce. "Be sure to watch Rags, Angel," she added, then slammed the door and was gone.

Angel yawned. There was nothing to do. She took a book from her bookshelf and paged through it. A picture of Marie Antoinette, the beautiful French queen, caught her eye. The jewels around her neck and on her long, flowing gown sparkled like tiny stars. Her hair was swept up into towering white curls piled high on top of her head. Angel wished she could be a queen like Marie Antoinette.

Rags came up the steps looking for her. "It's thundering out there," he said, "and lightning." Rags was afraid of thunder and lightning.

Angel held the book up so Rags could see the picture. "Look at this, Rags. Don't you wish we lived then? This is the way we would look."

Rags looked at the picture. "You could dress like that," said Rags. "You've got long skirts." He was remembering Halloween and how Angel had dressed them both like gypsies.

"Rags!" said Angel. "Let's dress up!"

Rags jumped up and down. He always liked Angel's ideas.

"I'll be Marie Antoinette, and you can be King Louis."

"King Louis," repeated Rags.

Angel looked at the book. "How can we get our hair white like that?" She had never seen any wigs in the house. "It looks powdered," she said, more to herself than to Rags. "Rags! We can powder our hair!" She ran to the bathroom for the can of talcum powder.

"Let's try it on your hair first," she said. "It's shorter." Angel sprinkled the talcum powder lightly over Rags's head. He sneezed. "It isn't staying," she said. "And it isn't really very white." Angel frowned. "We need something really white. What can you think of that is really white, Rags?"

"Flour," said Rags. "Flour is white."

Angel ran ahead of him down the stairs. They went to the kitchen and scooped two cups of flour from the can in the cupboard into a brown paper sack.

"Put your head in the bag, Rags."

"You're the one who wants to be Marie Antoinette."

"C'mon, Rags, we'll both do it. I'll do it after you."

She slipped the bag over Rags's head and shook it. Rags screamed. "Cut it out!" he called, in muffled tones. "Take it off."

When she did, his hair was white. His face and eyebrows and ears were white, too. "Oh Rags, it works!"

She put a little on a strand of her hair.

"C'mon, Angel, put your head in!" Rags brushed flour from his face. He looked in the oven door at his hair. It was very white.

Angel put her head carefully into the bag and shook it. When she took it out, Rags shook his head. "Not white enough," he said. She tried again. This time it was very, very white. Almost all the flour was gone. "Now I'll have to comb it high on my head," she said.

Angel and Rags ran back upstairs. Angel looked once more at the picture of Marie Antoinette, then sat down in front of the bathroom mirror. She swept her floury hair on top of her head and fastened it with barrettes.

"Now we need jewels!" she said.

"That old cat collar in the basement has jewels," said Rags.

Angel ran down the two flights of stairs to the basement and hunted through some cardboard storage cartons. "It's just right!" she said when she found it. She fastened the collar to the front of her hair. It sparkled brightly under the bathroom light. Angel got her mother's old eye makeup and worked on her face. When she was through, she turned her attention to Rags. "You don't look like Louis," she said, looking at the picture. "He has longer hair, Rags, and some kind of curls, like a permanent wave, on the sides...I think we should curl your hair."

"I don't want curls!" said Rags. "And I don't want white hair."

Angel stamped her foot. "You said you did!"

"No, I didn't. *You* did." He pointed a finger at Angel.

Angel remembered that she was the one who had suggested the white hair. She looked around the room for the first time since they began. "What a mess," she said to Rags. "Go get the broom. We have to clean this flour up."

They threw the paper sack away and swept the floors. Then they wiped the cupboards and stove. There seemed to be flour on everything, even in the bathroom. "Such a little bit of flour — how did it get on everything in the house?" she said.

When they finished cleaning, they went to look outdoors. The storm seemed to be just about over.

"I don't want white hair," said Rags again.

"Just brush it out then," said Angel impatiently. She'd lost interest in dressing up.

Rags got a hairbrush and began to brush. He brushed and brushed. "It's still white," he said.

"Brush it harder," said Angel, taking the barrettes out of her own hair and removing the jewels and pins. She got another hairbrush and began to brush her own hair, along with Rags. They both brushed and brushed, and they both still had white hair.

"My gosh," said Angel after a long time. "I guess we'll have to wash it out. Maybe we should wash it before Mom comes home."

They ran downstairs once more and filled the laundry tub with warm water. Then they bent over and soaked their heads in the tub. After they had scrubbed awhile, Angel turned off the water and looked at Rags. His hair was standing up in white sticky spikes all around his head. He looked like pictures she had seen of the Statue of Liberty.

"Rags?" she said. "I just remembered something."

"What?" said the Statue of Liberty.

"Do you remember how we make paste for our scrapbooks?"

Rags looked at Angel's hair. "We mix up flour and water in a big bowl," he said.

Angel nodded. "Flour and water. Flour and water together make paste." She looked into the shiny side of the washing machine. "Rags, what we have on our heads is paste."

Rags was silent for a while. Then he began to wail. "I don't want paste on my head," he said.

"Well, I don't either," said Angel crossly. "You aren't the only one, you know."

Angel looked around the basement. "I think we need soap," she said. She walked over to the shelf and took down the boxes of laundry soap and dry bleach and poured a little of the contents on their heads. "We need hotter water," she said. "Now *rub*, Rags," she added.

Both of them rubbed and rubbed. Their hair was still sticky. "We need something stronger," said Angel. Her glance fell on the bottle her mother used for ring-around-the-collar. "For stubborn stains," Angel read.

She carefully sprayed it first on Rags's hair, and then on her own. "We'll let it set awhile, the way Mom does for stains."

After five minutes Angel rubbed it in thoroughly and rinsed it out. She stepped back and looked at Rags. "I think that is the best we can do," she said. "It's pretty well out."

The two dried their hair with a towel and combed it. When they looked in a mirror, they saw that only a few spikes were left.

"It looks lighter," said Rags.

"That's because it's so clean," said Angel doubtfully.

Rags sniffed the air. "It smells," he said. "Our hair smells."

"It's the bleach," said Angel. "We'll spray it with perfume."

By the time their mother came home, they were sitting out on the back steps with dry hair. It had stopped raining completely now. Alyce and their mother unloaded the groceries from the car, and Angel carried the bags into the house.

"Can't you find anything to do, Angel?" said Mrs. O'Leary. Her glance seemed to rest on their heads for a minute. "I hate it when you don't use your imagination to keep busy. Now, come in the house and get out the flour. I'm going to make pork chops for dinner, and you can make the gravy."

THREE

Alyce's Free Offer

Angel stood before the hall mirror studying her hair. It was still stiff in some places from the flour. She had wet it in the morning as she combed it, but when it dried it stuck up in peaks again. Rags's hair seemed to have settled down. Maybe that was because he wore his baseball cap all the time.

As Angel stood there, Alyce bustled in carrying a box with some rattly things in it. "Good morning, Angel," she said, smiling past her.

Angel frowned. It wasn't a good morning. It

was no different from all the other mornings. She wondered why people never said "Bad morning" when they got up and "Bad night" when they went to bed. English was funny, she reflected. Someday she would make up a new language that made more sense. And all the words would be spelled the way they sounded, without letters thrown in to trick children in tests.

"Angel!" called her mother in a suspiciously pleasant voice. "Come here a minute, dear." When her mother called in that tone of voice, it usually meant she wanted Angel to do something she didn't want to do. Angel turned slowly and went into the dining room.

"Come right in," Mrs. O'Leary said, as if Angel were someone she had just met for the first time. "You'll never guess what! Alyce has offered to cut your hair! It's been so dingy looking lately and haircuts are so expensive. Isn't that nice of her, darling?"

Angel knew that old trick. Her mother always

brought up a disagreeable subject in front of someone else. It was impossible to argue. Angel wondered why rules for children were so different from grown-up rules. She remembered once when Rags had brought home a little friend and asked if he could stay for lunch. After he left, Mrs. O'Leary took Rags aside and said, "Rags, don't ever ask if someone can stay for lunch when he's standing right here. Then if I say no, it sounds rude." But now, here was her mother doing the same thing.

"I don't want my hair cut," Angel said on principle. She really didn't know if she wanted it cut or not.

"Why, sure you do, Angel. It's long and stringy and too hot for summer. It hangs down your neck and makes you uncomfortable." How could her mother know what she wanted? If Angel herself wasn't sure, how could her mother be? Her mother was smiling brightly, but there was a warning look in her eye.

Alyce was sharpening her scissors with something that looked like sandpaper. She laid out a comb and mirror and electric clippers. "Sit down, dear, said her mother, the edges of her smile beginning to straighten out. She tied a bathtowel around Angel's neck.

"I'm new at this, so we'll just go slowly," said Alyce, trying to sound as cheerful as possible.

"Oh no," groaned Angel, inside. "She's probably never cut hair before." She was using Angel to practice on. As if she knew what Angel was thinking, Alyce said, "I cut my nephew Harold's hair once, and it looked just fine."

Angel knew Harold. She had seen him in school. And she remembered his haircut. He came to school one day and everyone had laughed because his hair was so short, and in some places there was hardly any hair at all. His head had a funny shape, a bit pointed, and the teacher had warned the class when Harold went out for a drink of water, not to tease him. She said, "Boys and girls, Harold is embarrassed about his haircut. We all think it is very nice, don't we?" When Harold had come back into the room, the teacher said, "I like your haircut, Harold." Angel was sure she had been lying. No one could like that haircut. She wondered if it was all right to lie if there was a good reason, like making someone feel better, although she was sure Harold couldn't have been taken in. He must have had a mirror. He could see for himself how horrible he looked.

Now here was his aunt, ready to do the same kind of damage to Angel's hair. Maybe she should warn her mother about Harold before it was too late. But it *was* too late. Alyce had already begun to chip away at Angel's head. Angel felt like a piece of marble that a sculptor was working on. A nick here. A gash there. Chip, chip, chip. Pieces of marble flew to the floor. The sculptor stood back to look at her work. She frowned. But she couldn't start over; the nicks and gashes were there forever. Unless she took an entirely new piece of marble. And Angel didn't have another head.

"Sit up, Angel."

Chip, chip, chip. The marble flew. Then the sculptor tried a new tool. Carve, carve, carve. Angel felt her head getting smaller. Perhaps Alyce would chip and carve until Angel had a little tiny head on a large body. Or until she had no head at all! Once that had happened when Angel made a paper doll. She tried and tried to get the head the right shape, and the more she tried the more she cut, and the more she cut the smaller the doll's head had become, until she had to cut the whole body down to match and she had only a little wisp of a doll left. Before long, Angel knew she'd be too small to go to school again. She'd be a baby in a cradle and have to live all those long ten years over — the first day of school, all those days taking care of Rags. If she was lucky, that is. If not, she might be whittled away to nothing at all.

"Shorter!" said her mother, who liked to get her money's worth. She always got Angel's

clothes too big so that she could grow into them, but they wore out before they fit her. Angel was sure her mother felt the same way about haircuts. She wanted it cut short so that it would take a long time to grow and need to be cut again. At the word *shorter,* Alyce picked up the scissors and began all over again. Chip, chip, chip, clip, clip, clip, Angel made up a song, as hair, her own floured hair, tumbled down over her nose and onto the towel. Singing the song inside her head made her sleepy, and the sleepier she got the more she dreamed she was whittled away to nothing. Just when she thought nothing was left but her mind, and no one could see her, they could only hear her, Alyce's voice roused her.

"That should do!" she said, as she took the towel off Angel's shoulders. Then she combed and plucked and powdered Angel's neck the way barbers do. Brushing her off with a whisk broom, she handed Angel the mirror.

"You look like a waif, a dear little waif!" said her mother.

"She looks like Julie Andrews in *The Sound of Music*!" said Alyce.

Angel looked. She had been right. Her head was smaller. And her ears were larger. It was worse than she had imagined. She had almost no hair! Rags's face, pressed against the screen in the door, had a look of horror on it, worse than if he had laughed. Angel put the mirror down on the table and ran out the door.

Outside, she kept running, with Rags following her. "Where are we going?" said Rags.

Then Rags knew. They were going under the porch. Under the back porch was where they went to get away from adults. There was a wooden latticework wall hanging down from the porch floor, and when they lifted up one section they could crawl into a very private place. It was dark and quiet sitting on the cool ground among the old ladders and rakes that were stored there. When Angel was small she had tried to dig a hole to China from under the porch. She was too old for that now, but she still occasionally sat in the secret place where no adults would fit.

She ran her hand over her head. It felt bald. All she could feel was ears. Angel had no friends as it was, she surely wouldn't find any looking like this. Who would want to be friends with someone who had no hair? She would have cried, but she felt too bad even for that. She looked longingly at Rags's locks, curling over his ears. She had never noticed before how much hair he had. It looked thick and shiny and stood high on his head and hung down onto his neck.

"Oh Rags, what am I going to *do?*"

"Will it come back?" he said.

"Not for years," said Angel.

"I can see lots of your face," said Rags, encouragingly.

"Lots of ears," said Angel. "My ears stick out."

"They stick way out," agreed Rags.

Angel hadn't expected such quick agreement. She had hoped Rags would say he hadn't noticed and felt angry at him for his honesty. Rags was humming now and making small roads in the dirt for his toy cars. He had a village chiseled into the dirt and every so often he added something new — a road, a tree, a house.

"What should we do with my ears?" said Angel.

Rags looked thoughtful. "We could glue them to your head. That would be better," he said.

"Ha, ha," said Angel, who still had the flour-water paste in her mind. She didn't think any mention of glue was funny.

Angel and Rags heard footsteps over their heads. "Where do you suppose the children went?" their mother was saying to Alyce.

"Probably around the block," said Alyce. "Angel is no doubt showing off her new haircut. Don't worry about them so much. You really shouldn't be so overprotective. They need to go off and make friends."

Angel's mother quickly changed the subject. "The haircut's a fine job, Alyce," her mother was saying. "In fact, I think I'd like to surprise Angel and take her to the city to have her picture taken. Maybe Angel and Rags together, for Christmas cards."

Angel shivered. Never, she thought. Never would she be in a picture, preserved forever in their album without hair. Never would she come out from under the porch. Even if she starved to death. Well, Rags could bring her food. She could picture her mother and Rags eating all alone at the large table in the dining room . . . missing her, and talking about the fine times they all used to have. And Rags smuggling food into his pocket from his plate to take to her after dark.

The footsteps went down the porch stairs and a voice called good-bye. Mrs. O'Leary went into the house.

"Rags, I'm never coming out of here. Never. I don't want anyone to see me with no hair and a small head and big ears. Don't you ever tell Mom where I am. Promise, Rags, and hope to die."

Rags clamped his hand over his chest and crossed his heart and hoped to die. "I won't tell," he said. "But Mom will find you," he added. "She'll get everyone we know to look. Maybe she'll even call the police." His eyes grew large at the word *police.*

Angel ran her hands up through her hair from the bottom up. It felt like someone's beard. Maybe if she kept pushing it up instead of down it would stand out, away from her head. She realized that Rags was right. Their mother would find her. She was not likely to say, "Oh, it's too bad we lost Angel," and go about her shopping and cleaning as usual. Angel had a feeling she could never get lost, even if she set her mind to it. Even if she ran away. Their mother never lost anything. Especially her children. Angel thought again of what Alyce had said. Maybe she wasn't so bad after all. She did notice how unusual it was for Angel not to have a friend her own age.

"Rags," said Angel suddenly. "Go to my room

and get my red sweatshirt. It's in my closet on the floor."

"Are you cold?" asked Rags.

"Just go get it!" said Angel. She would have stamped her foot but she wasn't standing up. It was too low under the porch to stand up.

Rags wiped his hands on his shirt and crawled out from under the latticework. In a few minutes he was back with the sweatshirt. Angel put it on over her shirt and flung the attached hood over her head. She tied the string tightly under her chin and crawled out of the secret place into the bright sunlight. Rags followed her to the back steps, where they sat with their chins in their hands watching the cars go by. Before long it was lunchtime. Their mother came out looking for them.

"Oh, there you are!" she said. "Angel, what-ever are you doing in that hooded sweatshirt?"

"I like it," said Angel.

Her mother looked at the thermometer. "It's seventy-five degrees," she said. "You must be coming down with something. Do you feel chilled, dear? Do you feel sick?"

Angel did feel sick. She felt sad and lonely and ugly and her stomach felt awful too. "No," she said to her mother.

She ate lunch with her sweatshirt on and dinner with it on and the next morning she put it on over her sundress, despite her mother's protests. She was very warm but her head wasn't naked and fuzzy anymore. Fall was bound to come soon, and she could wear her hooded sweatshirt to school. No one need ever know that her head wasn't the right size.

FOUR

Angel Breaks the Law

Angel was wearing her red sweatshirt, idly watching Rags peel bark off a birch twig.

"I could make a canoe," he said. "An Indian canoe."

"You'd need more bark," said Angel, whose mind was on her hair, which wasn't growing back very quickly. Before long fall would come, and if the October winds blew her hood off, her head would be exposed and everyone would laugh. She tightened the string beneath her chin and decided to get some hair tonic at the drugstore if she ever had a chance to get there without her mother. She probably never would have a chance. The thought made her angry.

"There's a whole tree full of bark," said Rags, pointing.

"You can't take bark off a tree. It's illegal."

"It's our tree."

"Doesn't matter," she snapped at Rags. "Besides, the tree would die. A tree dies when its bark is gone."

Rags began to pout. It seemed that every time he had a good idea for something there was a law or a sign or some good reason why he couldn't follow through on it. He told Angel this.

Angel was in the mood to take action. "Just once, I'd like to do exactly the opposite of what all those signs and labels say," she said. Her eyes lit up with the thought of retaliation for the short haircut. Rags caught her spirit of rebellion.

"Angel?" he daringly said. "Let's use the rug cleaner on glass."

Angel looked at him. Their mother had gone to a garage sale this morning. It might be a good time to break the law. It was just a little law anyway. When Angel helped clean the house every Saturday, she read the labels on bottles to Rags. DO NOT USE ON GLASS! was the warning on the can of Gumption. "Safe for wool, polyester, vinyl, leather, cotton, and rayon. Do not use on glass." Every time Angel read the label, a chill went down her spine. She had always wanted to use the cleaner on glass. Now was as good a time as any.

She and Rags raced to the kitchen where they quickly found the Gumption.

"What do you suppose could happen?" she said, in a whisper.

Rags shrugged his shoulders. "Maybe it will explode," he said hopefully. "Like firecrackers on the Fourth of July."

"Maybe it will eat the glass all up," said Angel. "Maybe it will make a hole right through the window."

She decided the window in the kitchen would be a good place to try it. Just in case it did eat up the glass, they could pull down the shade and the hole wouldn't show. They would use only a little to test it. It would probably make just a tiny hole.

They sat down at the kitchen table and looked at the can.

"Are you sure we should do it, Rags?" said Angel.

Rags nodded his head vigorously. Nothing much had happened this summer. They had to take their excitement where they could find it. It might be right here inside this can.

"All right, then," said Angel. "If you think so."

At the window, Angel took off the cap and pointed the nozzle. She pressed a button. A thick flow of white sudsy foam came out, frosting the glass.

"It looks like Christmas!" said Rags, jumping up and down. They stood and looked at the foam. It clung to the window and then began

to run down in small rivulets. They watched it
for a long time.

Rags grew impatient. "When is something
going to happen?" he said.

Angel sprayed a little more on the window.

Still nothing happened. She sprayed a whole lot on and they waited some more. The suds ran down and formed a puddle at their feet.

"Nothing," said Angel. "Nothing."

Rags stamped his foot. "Why do they write things on bottles for nothing?"

Angel was angry, too. Why did the can warn them about glass when nothing happened to it at all? It was bad enough for *people* to lie; now it seemed she couldn't believe labels either. Angel got a paper towel and wiped the Gumption off the floor and the window. It didn't all come off, so she wiped some more.

"Look at that," said Rags, whistling between his teeth. He had just learned to do that. "It left a mark." He was right. No matter how hard Angel rubbed, she couldn't wipe away the long, colored streaks that looked like the patterns on her mother's good dishes or the puddle of gas at the filling station when it rained.

"It looks pretty!" said Rags. "Don't people like colored windows in their houses? You can see rainbows," he added.

Angel sighed. The Gumption didn't eat the window and make a hole. But colored windows were better than nothing. She pulled down the shade and tried to think of a more exciting rule to disobey.

"Let's take the 'Don't-remove-this-tag-under-penalty-of-law' tag off the mattress!" she said.

Rags ran ahead of Angel up the stairs. He pulled the blanket and spread off his bed and recited the warning that Angel had read to him many times in the past. "Do not remove this tag under penalty of law." It sounded very official. He and Angel had always been tempted to give it a good swift pull when they changed the sheets on the bed, but they never did because the sign said not to.

"I'm tired of these warnings," said Angel. Rags watched as she took one end and pulled it. It was sewed tightly. She pulled again. At last the label came off.

"Do you think anyone saw us?" whispered Rags.

"Who would see us?" said Angel.

"A policeman," whispered Rags.

Angel went into her own room and removed the tag on her mattress.

"I don't think we should take Mom's off. She wouldn't like us messing up her bed," said Rags.

"I know where there are more!" said Angel, running back down the stairs.

She went into the living room and grabbed the two sofa pillows. "Now!" she said.

"Read it first!" ordered Rags.

"Do not remove under penalty of law."

Rags shivered. It gave him a bit of a scare to tangle with the law. He pulled the tags off.

"All our life," said Angel, pulling off another tag, "we've done what signs said."

"Not anymore!" said Rags, with enthusiasm.

"Well," said Angel, "not today anyway." But now, hearing Rags's words —"Not anymore!"— she suddenly remembered that she was responsible for him. She pictured him in the future, crossing railroad tracks where it said

DO NOT CROSS HERE! and swimming where it said DEEP WATER, KEEP OUT! She saw Rags as a young man, striking a match with the cover of the matchbook open, when it said CLOSE BEFORE STRIKING. She saw him trampled by a bull when he opened a gate with a sign that said KEEP OUT.

Angel shivered. Now the picture came to her of Rags, an old man, driving a car on the left side of the road when the sign said KEEP RIGHT!

"Look Angel," she heard him say in the future. "See that sign? I never do what signs say!" She saw Rags behind the wheel of a car, still short but with a mustache, waving to her as he entered an off ramp with a sign that said WRONG WAY and had a red slash through it.

"*Stop!*" she called to Rags. At this rate Rags would never live to be an old man with a mustache, or even a young man. His short life would soon be over, and it would be all Angel's fault.

She pictured Rags being pulled from deep water. A crowd was gathering and everyone was pointing at Angel. "It's her! She's the one responsible for his life!" they called. Her mother was crying into her handkerchief and the policeman was getting out his handcuffs. The crowd in the background was booing. Angel felt heartbroken. Rags only had one life and it was over. There wasn't another chance. All because Angel used Gumption on glass and showed Rags how to remove tags illegally.

Angel opened her eyes. She was relieved to see her little brother still sitting on the floor, folding the tags into airplanes and canoes.

"*Rags!*" she said, throwing her arms around his small healthy body. Rags looked surprised. "I'm sorry I told you to do this!" she said. She was so relieved to see him breathing and well that she resolved never to misdirect him again.

"Let's clean all this stuff up," she said.

"Aw," said Rags, "I wanted to put Mom's cactus in the shade." Angel knew which cactus he meant. It had a sign stuck in its pot that said KEEP IN A SUNNY PLACE. DO NOT OVERWATER. Angel had read it to him yesterday.

"No!" shouted Angel. "I don't think it's a good

idea to disobey signs," she added in a quieter voice. "Just forget all those signs I've been reading to you, Rags. We aren't going to play that game anymore. You may never get to kindergarten this fall if we do. Come on, let's put these pillows back."

Rags looked disappointed. Angel kept chattering all the time she was straightening up. Sisters were funny, he thought.

"...and stay out of deep water," she was saying.

He wondered if a brother would be like this. She was going on and on now about driving on the right side of the road. Just a minute ago they were having such fun, breaking rules.

"Do you know your right hand from your left, Rags? Hold your right hand up for me." When did children learn left and right? Maybe in kindergarten. Well, that should be soon enough...maybe she should teach him herself now just to be sure... Angel was thinking once again what a bother Rags was, when their mother came in. She gave them both a kiss.

"See what I got at the sale!" she said. She rattled a box with loose things in it. "A barbecue grill! We can cook outside with it. The only thing is, it has to be assembled. It has directions right on this tag. All the rules. You just have to do what it says. Do you think you could put it together, Angel? You and Rags?"

Angel took the box from her mother. "We can do it," she said. "We read instructions on things all the time." She gave Rags a warning look.

"Well, good," said Mrs. O'Leary, brightly. "That's a good habit." She patted Rags on the head and went to the kitchen to make a cup of tea. Mom would never know, Angel thought, how grateful she should be that Rags was alive.

FIVE

Angel to the Rescue

The barbecue grill was put together, and they had cooked supper on it twice. Angel's hair was at last beginning to cover her ears again, and she had abandoned her sweatshirt. Her head felt natural now, perhaps because she was used to short hair, but she was staying well out of the range of Alyce and her scissors.

One afternoon her mother called to her, "Angel, I'm going to work now! Don't go off the block, or leave burners on, or cross any streets. And be sure to keep your eye on Rags every minute. It only takes a second for someone to be hit by a car. Angel? Did you hear me?"

Angel heard her mother. She called "Yes" and said good-bye to her. It was going to be a long afternoon. She made a peanut butter sandwich for herself and one for Rags and then went out to the back yard to call her brother. He was next door, walking through the Bagleys' yard. Angel could see him clearly from where she sat. He stopped at the Bagleys' TV antenna, a large one that was set on four big poles on the ground and rose alongside the Bagleys' two-story house higher than the roof. Rags was swinging around the poles and singing. Angel finished her sandwich and walked over to join him. By the time she got there, Rags had his foot on the lowest rung of the antenna. By the time she had brushed all the crumbs off her jeans, Rags was on the fourth rung.

"Come on," he said. "It's like a ladder. It's for climbing."

Angel looked up through the maze of steel at

the blue sky. She had seen Mr. Bagley climb up a short way to adjust something so that they could see TV better. She supposed it was for climbing, like a ladder. It was a fancy jungle gym. Angel climbed up to where Rags was so that he wouldn't fall. They took one more step each. Then another.

"Look," said Rags, before long. He was holding on with one hand and pointing with the other. Angel looked down to the ground where he was pointing. They had come much farther than she thought.

"Oh my," she said. "Rags, maybe we better go back down."

But Rags was already scampering up higher, and in order to guard his life, Angel climbed right behind him.

"Rags!" called Angel. "Stop right there!"

Now the wind was blowing and Rags could not hear her. "Rags!" she called again. She looked over her shoulder. She could see the roof of their own house! She had never seen the top of their roof before. She saw her blue Frisbee, and a ball in the gutter. She could see the tops of cars, as well, in fact the top of everything: trees, people's heads, garages, churches, even the post office. This view was certainly different from the one she had from her back steps, or even the oil truck.

Angel suddenly wished her feet were on the ground, and that Rags's feet were on the ground with hers. She turned and looked over her head. Rags was at the top now, sitting on the edge of the wide antenna platform. He wasn't smiling. "I don't like it up here," he said as Angel came closer. "It's too high."

"Of course it's too high," said Angel matter-of-factly, trying to sound calm. She had heard how dangerous it was to panic in an emergency.

"We'll just go right back down and you'll feel better." Angel took a step down. Rags didn't follow. He looked as though he was going to cry.

"Did you hear me? We'll just go right back down, Rags. Just like we came up."

"I can't," said Rags.

Angel was quiet, thinking hard. "Of course you can," she said. "Just follow me."

Angel lowered her foot and felt for the next rung. It wasn't nearly as easy as coming up. She got a nervous feeling in the pit of her stomach that Rags could never find the rungs, going backward with his short little legs. "C'mon," she called lightly. "There's nothing to it," she lied.

By now Rags's frown had turned to sobs. Angel hated to give up the progress she had made going down, but she quickly climbed up again to where Rags sat at the very top. The wind whipped around both their heads. Angel sat down on the edge of the platform across from Rags to think some more. She certainly couldn't carry him down; it was hard enough to get herself down, and she needed both hands to hold on to the sides. She wanted to dash down as fast as she could, herself, and forget this whole thing ever happened, but of course she couldn't leave Rags high atop an antenna, all alone in the sky.

She looked down. A crowd was beginning to gather. Anxious faces were looking up at them. Her mind flashed to a scene from a program she had seen on television, in which a man balanced four pop bottles on a long board suspended out of a high window. On the pop bottles he put a chair, one leg in each bottle. On top of that he put another chair. Then, as a deep voice called for silence, the man stood on his hands on the top chair, high above the noisy street, without a net. Angel pictured herself now, bowing, first to one side and then the other. Suddenly she stopped and scolded herself. How could she play games when Rags's life was in danger, to say nothing of her own? The people below seemed to be calling out words, hands around their mouths forming the shape of a megaphone, but the words must have blown away on the wind. Angel didn't really want to know what they were saying, anyway. It wouldn't help.

Her mother appeared in the crowd below. She must be home from work already! Mrs. O'Leary was pointing to the ground over and

over again. Now Angel felt as though she was playing charades at a birthday party. She wanted to lean over and spell out the word: G-R-O-U-N-D. Yes, I know the answer. Ground. Get down here on the ground. But what good did it do to know the answer? She was as far from the ground as ever.

"Maybe we should jump," said Rags, whose tears had dried now that he saw that Angel was not leaving him and that some sort of party was forming below for his benefit.

"You'd be dead, just like that." Angel snapped her fingers. She was tired of being nice to Rags. He got them into this mess and should know the hard facts. She wished she could abandon him this very minute. Maybe she could run away to Australia and start a new life, one without a brother. Instead, she said, "Can't you turn around carefully and follow me down, Rags? Then we'd all be safe and we could go in the house and watch TV. I made a peanut butter sandwich for you."

Rags didn't hear anything after "turn around carefully." At that point, he began to wail again, more loudly now.

"All right," said Angel angrily. "Stay there. Just hold on, and stop screaming. Someone will do something. I hope."

Angel both hoped and feared they would do something. It was hard to imagine what it might be. Anything that would get Rags down from this antenna was bound to get her deeper into trouble.

Suddenly there was new action on the ground. A man appeared carrying a long extension ladder. With great fanfare the man placed the ladder against the side of the antenna. He positioned it so that its feet were firm, and then he started climbing. Angel couldn't see who it was, but she guessed it was probably Mr. Bagley. Her mother was wringing her hands now. Angel could see that the ladder did not go far enough. It stopped far below her. When Mr. Bagley got to the top of the ladder, he said, "Can you come down this far, Angel?"

"I can, but Rags can't," said Angel, having to shout even at this distance.

Mr. Bagley scratched his head. "This antenna may not bear my weight," he called. "See if you can persuade Rags to come down a little way."

"Rags," she coaxed him. "You can have a candy bar if you come down."

Rags repeated his screaming. When the cries subsided, Angel said, "Rags, if you don't try to come down from here you are going to starve to death, and I am going down without you."

Angel made up her mind. She was through with Rags. She turned around to do as she had threatened.

Rags suddenly stood up and put his feet on the rungs. He began to lower himself, rung by rung. It took a minute or two for his feet to find a place, but before long he reached the ladder. Angel went the rest of the way down the antenna, while Mr. Bagley put Rags under one arm and climbed carefully down the ladder, holding on with his other hand.

Angel's mother, who looked as if she had

been crying herself, gathered the tearful Rags into her arms and thanked Mr. Bagley. She was apologizing over and over again as people started to wander back to their own homes. After Mr. Bagley lowered his ladder and carried it away, Angel waited for her mother to say, "Angel, why did you ever do a thing like that?" but she didn't. Instead, she hugged them close to her and said with tears in her eyes, "You and Rags could have been killed."

Angel nodded her head.

"I don't know how it happened," Mrs. O'Leary said. "I don't even want to know. We will just put it out of our minds and hope that you have learned from this awful experience." Then she went to lie down on her bed with a cold cloth on her forehead.

Angel and Rags returned to their yard. Later, Angel watched as Mr. Bagley erected a sign beside the TV antenna that said, DANGER, KEEP OFF. She thought to herself, "What good will that do? Rags can't even read yet." But deep down, she knew that she was in charge of reading for both of them. She frowned. She hoped she could keep Rags healthy, or at least alive, until he started kindergarten in the fall. Right now she felt that she was the one who would never survive. Every one of her problems could be traced to Rags. No, she thought, she could never wait until he was in school. Something needed to be done about Rags *now.*

SIX

Mall Trouble

Angel was taking an orange from the refrigerator when her mother came into the kitchen. "Since I have the day off today, dear, I thought we could go to the new shopping mall and get you and Rags some fall clothes." Angel looked up in surprise. It sounded like a good idea. A chance to get away from her house, away from her boring street. But then she thought of Rags. Rags holding her hand. Rags sticky from lollipops that people gave children in malls. Rags asking questions. But most of all, Rags would probably get her into some kind of mall trouble — even worse than the trouble she had gotten into when they climbed the Bagleys' antenna.

"Let's leave Rags home," she said.

Her mother looked shocked. "Where would we leave him, Angel? And besides, he has to try clothes on to be sure they fit. I can't get shoes for him if he doesn't come."

Angel's spirits fell. Wherever she went, Rags was at her heels. She felt as if there was some rope attached from him to her, an invisible rope that was strong and unbreakable, pulling, always pulling, at her waist. Rags pulling at her in the mall was no different from his pulling at her around the block.

"Go and wash up, dear, and comb your hair. I'll get Rags and clean him up."

Mrs. O'Leary went out to the porch to call Rags. He was excited about going to the mall, as Angel knew he would be. Things were far more fun when you were four, she thought. No one expected a thing of four-year-olds. They didn't have to take care of anyone, not even themselves.

Angel threw water on her face and combed her hair. A few minutes later, Rags was ready, too, his face shiny and red, and his hair with fresh comb marks still in it. Their mother sat in front of them in the bus, and Angel was left victim to Rags's pestering. She stared out the window at the passing farms and tried to think of a way to get back at her mother for saddling her with this four-year-old, a way to get back at Rags. By the time they arrived at the mall, Angel was still thinking, and hadn't come up with any answer.

"Now," said Mrs. O'Leary. "We'll check the sales at Dayton's first." At Dayton's, she bought Angel underwear for school and a warm cap and a plaid jacket that Angel didn't like very much, but it was serviceable and it was on sale. She bought Rags new corduroy overalls and a pair of blue sneakers. Then, just as Angel had feared, her mother said: "Now that that's done, I'm going to look at the dresses at Humminger's.

You and Rags go down and visit the animals in the petting zoo, Angel. Rags will like that. And keep your eye on him every minute. I wouldn't know where to start looking if, God forbid, he should get lost in a mall this size. I'll meet you at two o'clock in front of Teasley's." At these last few words, her mother pointed to Teasley's and the door where she would be. Then she set off in the direction of Humminger's.

Rags reached for Angel's hand and pulled her toward the zoo. But Angel held back. She didn't want to go to the zoo. She had seen baby farm animals plenty of times. Besides, she was too old to pet baby animals. It was time she did something *she* wanted to do. And what she wanted to do now was be rid of Rags. She pulled her hand out of his and said loudly, "Quit hanging on to me, for Pete's sake! I don't want to see the animals. I want to look in the store windows."

At this news, Rags began to whimper. "Let's go to the zoo," he wailed. "I want to see the animals."

Angel stamped her foot. "Grow up, Rags. I'm not going to see the animals and that's that."

Rags whined, but Angel ignored him and turned to look into the window where she had seen a display of summer sandals at half price. She pretended he wasn't with her. She kept pretending that he wasn't with her as she moved down the mall, looking in the windows of other stores, and suddenly he wasn't.

Just a moment before, Angel had seen him swinging from a railing around a small fountain, but when she turned around a moment later to say, "Come on, Rags, we'll get an ice cream cone at Busby's," he didn't answer. Angel quickly glanced around between the busy shoppers, sure that her eye would light on Rags's red shirt with the elephants marching around the collar. She didn't see it.

She turned and looked in the other direction. No Rags.

"Good grief," she said out loud in a bored voice, with just a tinge of panic beginning to creep in.

73

With a casual air, Angel looked into the doorways of the stores nearby. She retraced her steps to the sandal store. "It would serve him right if he was lost for good," she muttered. Then she pictured herself at two o'clock, meeting her mother at Teasley's — alone. She imagined the long ride home with no Rags, and life with her mother, bereft of Rags. She felt mixed emotions.

Suddenly real panic set in. Angel flew across the mall, from store to store, up the steps and down, searching for the red shirt. This, then, was what her mother had dreaded. She finally had fulfilled her mother's prophecy: she had not kept her eye on Rags; she had lost him. Forever.

She saw a postman unlocking a box for a mail pickup. He was whistling and looked happy. How could he be happy when Rags was gone forever? She ran up to him and asked with a shaky voice, "Have you seen a little boy in a red shirt?"

She crossed her fingers, hoping that he knew exactly where Rags was and would tell her. Then she would simply go to that spot, chastise Rags, and meet her mother with her little brother in tow.

The mailman stopped whistling. "Sorry," he said. "Where did you lose him?"

"I don't know," sobbed Angel. "I just turned away for a minute, and he was gone."

The mailman shook his head. "Got to keep your eye on those little ones," he said. "They get away fast."

Angel tore down the mall, between women with shopping bags and teenagers trying on eye makeup. Everyone looked so *happy* — so interested in unimportant things like hair ribbons and bedspreads. What could these things possibly matter?

Suddenly she remembered how Rags wanted to see the animals. "That's it!" she shouted. "He went to the zoo."

Relief spread over Angel. She sped down the steps to the first level, where the zoo was. From one pen to another she raced, looking for anything red.

"Have you seen a little boy in a red shirt?" she asked a woman with a little girl.

"I don't think so," said the woman.

Angel sat down on a bench, put her head in her hands, and cried.

"Dear me," said the woman. "I'm sure you'll find him. Children get lost here every day. Why don't you go to the manager's office and report a lost child?"

Angel looked up, surprised, as the woman pointed the way to the office.

"Thank you very much," said Angel, starting off in the direction the woman had pointed to. She was not very hopeful. Children may get lost every day, and found again, but Angel knew that Rags was lost forever. It was her punishment for hating her brother. Her mother always said that no bad deed went unpunished. People got found out sooner or later. Well, at last she, Angel, was found out. She was a person no one could trust. She was a selfish person, thinking only of herself. Her mother would be justified, no matter what awful way she punished her.

As Angel rounded the corner where the arrow pointed to OFFICE, she saw the mall exit to the parking lot.

"Oh, no! What if Rags left the mall!" thought Angel out loud. "He could walk out any door, into the parking lot."

Rags liked to explore. If he wasn't at the zoo, surely he had left to find more exciting things. At this very moment, he might be sauntering along the freeway, picking up a shiny rock or two, putting them into his pocket. Or perhaps he had gone downtown, to look up at the capitol from the bottom of the high steps. Her mother was right; it was impossible to know where to begin to look. Angel hated to know that her mother was always right.

She knocked on the office door. When a voice said "Come in," Angel burst through the door and cried, "I've lost my little brother!"

A tall, smiling man in a uniform got up from behind a desk and said calmly, "We'll find him;

just tell me what he was wearing and any other distinguishing features."

Although she knew she would never see Rags again, she was somewhat encouraged by the man's attitude.

"Name?" said the man. He had sat down behind the desk again and taken out a piece of paper and a pencil.

"Rags," said Angel.

The man looked up questioningly.

"Well, his real name is Theodore, but we call him Rags because of the ragged blanket he used to carry."

The officer frowned and wrote down RAGS on the piece of paper. "Now, what was he wearing?" he asked.

It was painful for Angel to describe Rags and his gone-forever outfit.

"A red T-shirt with elephants on the collar," she said. "And navy blue shorts. I think." Angel discovered that she wasn't sure of everything Rags was wearing. Well, if he ever came back, she would know what he was wearing, all the time. "And I think little red tennis shoes," she added. "He has light brown hair and brown eyes."

The officer picked up a microphone and flipped a switch. "Attention, please," he announced. "A little boy is lost." The words bounced out over the entire mall. "His name is Rags, and he is wearing navy blue shorts and a red shirt. Would anyone seeing him bring him to the office at the north end of the mall. Thank you." The man switched the microphone off. "Now," he said, "you just sit there and wait. Someone will bring him along in a little while."

Angel sank down into the chair the man had pointed to. She found it hard to believe that only this morning she had tried to think of ways to get even with her mother and Rags. She vowed that if she ever saw Rags alive again, she would not blame him for her problems. After all, he wouldn't be four all of his life.

Angel was so deep in thought about Rags and

her mother that for a moment she thought she heard their voices. She could almost hear Rags sob, "Where's Angel? I want Angel." The voice got louder and louder until, suddenly, Rags was standing right in front of her! He threw his arms around Angel and said, "Why did you get lost?"

Then Angel heard the clickety-click of her mother's heels, and before she knew it all of them were gathered in the mall office right in front of the officer's desk. Rags was found, just as the man had told her he would be.

"Rags!" shouted Angel. "Where were you?"

"He was with me," said Angel's mother. "We thought *you* were lost! Imagine our surprise when we heard the loudspeaker say Rags was lost, and to look for a little boy in a red shirt."

"I wasn't lost," said Rags. "Angel was lost."

"Well, whatever happened, it's all cleared up now," said Mrs. O'Leary, trying to calm everyone down.

Angel hugged Rags tightly to her. How could she ever have wanted him to go away? Then she hugged her mother. She even hugged the officer.

On the way home, they rode in silence, Rags cuddled down beside Angel, asleep. Suddenly her mother's voice broke through the stillness. "Perhaps you *are* with Rags too much," she said.

"Nonsense," said Angel, sounding for a moment like her mother. "I like being with Rags."

She had never said anything more truthful in her life.

SEVEN

Anything Goes

It was a long time before Angel let Rags out of her sight again. Her mother rarely told her now to "keep her eye" on Rags, but Angel did. She never took her eye off Rags. Many times, if she could, Mrs. O'Leary took Rags along with her to the supermarket and other places. Angel found out she even missed him when he was gone.

One afternoon when her mother was about to leave for work, she came out to the back porch looking for Angel. "Are you sure you can handle Rags?" she asked.

Angel nodded. "Of course," she said.

"Where *is* Rags, by the way?" said her mother.

Rags tapped on the porch floor to remind her not to give away their hiding place.

"He's . . . around."

Mrs. O'Leary glanced nervously down the street toward the Bagleys' TV antenna. "He's in the yard," said Angel. "Hiding."

"Oh," said her mother, looking satisfied. "That's fine, dear. Don't do anything that is . . . upsetting, while I'm gone," she said. "Alyce and I are going to stop off at the new market on the way home," she called out as she left.

Upsetting, thought Angel. So often things turned out to be upsetting when they began as something good. Angel tried to think of what she and Rags could do that would not be upsetting. Something that would please her mother. Something that, once she came in and saw it, would make her say, "Why Angel, what a fine non-upsetting thing to come home to! What would I do without you?"

Then her mother would hug her and tell her what a joy she was. How grown-up and mature. Instead of putting her lips together tightly and saying, "We'll just pretend this never happened."

"Rags?" called Angel. "What do you think we could do that Mom would like?"

Rags came out from under the porch with dirt on his knees and hands and face. He looked puzzled, as if he couldn't quite picture their doing something his mother would like.

"Well?" said Angel. "What would Mom like?"

"A present?" asked Rags cautiously.

Angel shook her head. "It can't be something we *buy*," she said. "It should be something we *do*."

Rags looked relieved. He didn't have much money, and it was much easier for him to think of doing something than of buying something.

"Vacuum?" said Rags. Rags liked to vacuum.

Angel shrugged her shoulders. "That's not special," she said. "We vacuum a lot. I want to do something that will be...noticed. Something that will turn out good."

"A cake?" ventured Rags. Turning out good reminded him of cakes.

Angel opened her eyes wider. "Well, maybe not a cake, but we could cook supper! Mom would notice that! We never did that before, Rags."

Angel pictured her mother coming home after work. As she came up the sidewalk, she would sniff the aroma of dinner cooking. She would think, "What smells so good, I wonder," and she would think it was coming from Margaret Toomer's house, behind them. "Can I be in the right house?" she would say. Then Angel would hand her a glass of Mountain Mist with two cherries in it and tell her to sit down. She would offer her mother the evening paper and push over the hassock for her feet. She would even serve her dinner on a tray in the living room instead of in the kitchen, and if the evening grew cool she would turn on the artificial fireplace and they all could sit together eating dinner, with a dog at their feet. Angel caught herself. They didn't have a dog, she remembered.

Rags interrupted this scene, saying, "What kind of supper?" He was saying it over and over. Angel hadn't stopped to think what kind of supper.

"Something that smells good cooking. Something we can make now and let cook in a pot, like Margaret Toomer does. We want it to smell like Margaret's house."

Angel got up and ran into the house with Rags right behind her. They opened the refrigerator and looked in. They saw four potatoes and a half can of soup and some peas that Rags didn't finish the evening before. There was also a can of anchovies swimming in oil that her mother liked to put on pizzas.

"Nothing in here smells good," said Rags.

"We have to cook it first to make it smell," said Angel. "Even I know that. Cold things don't smell."

Rags tried to remember that. He always tried to remember everything that Angel told him, like what the labels on things said. "Cold things don't smell, cold things don't smell," he said to himself over and over now, squeezing his eyes shut to help him remember better. It seemed to him that there was so much to learn that was brand new every day, he'd never be able to remember everything. His mind wasn't big enough.

Angel opened the hydrator pan. Lying forlornly at the bottom were three slightly shriveled carrots and some limp celery.

"I know!" said Angel. "We'll make stew!"

"Stew!" said Rags, jumping up and down. Then he frowned. "What's stew?"

"It's where you put everything together into one pot and its got gravy on it and it smells good because it cooks all day."

"You can put anything in it?" asked Rags.

"Anything goes in stew," said Angel, waving her hand across the contents of the refrigerator. "First, we have to wash our hands."

Angel scrubbed her hands with soap, and then she scrubbed Rags's.

"Now, we need a big pot," she said. She took her mother's Crockpot off the shelf and plugged it in. "You wash the vegetables, Rags. They have to be very clean before we put them in."

Angel and Rags took everything out of the refrigerator and washed it and put it into the Crockpot.

"Should we wash the anchovies?" asked Rags, from his place at the sink.

"No," said Angel. "You don't wash stuff in cans."

"You don't wash stuff in cans, you don't wash stuff in cans," sang Rags over and over to himself, with his eyes squeezed shut to block out all distractions. He put the anchovies into the pot.

"Onion," said Angel. "I know stew needs onion." She found one and cut it up.

"Anything-stew!" said Rags. "We're making anything-stew."

After they had put everything from the refrigerator into the pot, Angel remembered something else. "You need meat in stew," she said.

"Meat?" said Rags. "Why?"

"Because that's what stew has," said Angel. "Stew meat." She opened the freezer and a package of frankfurters fell out.

"Hot dogs!" shouted Rags. "Hot dogs are meat, aren't they, Angel?"

"Yes, they are meat—" said Angel. She closed her eyes and tried to remember if frankfurters were what she had seen in stew. She couldn't seem to see anything in her mind's eye except carrots. Carrots and gravy. She couldn't remember *not* seeing frankfurters in stew, so she began to cut them up with a sharp knife. As she cut them, Rags popped them into the Crockpot.

"Anything-stew," sang Rags, "has anything in it, in it, in it. When will it start to smell good, Angel?"

"Not yet," said Angel, turning up the control on the Crockpot from simmer low to simmer high. She took her big metal spoon and stirred all the things in the pot.

"Where's the gravy?" said Rags, looking over the edge.

"I don't know," said Angel. She was wondering the same thing. How did her mother get gravy around the stew? "I thought it just *came,*" she said to Rags. She stirred and stirred the stew. She and Rags stared into the pot.

"Maybe we have to put gravy in," said Rags.

"But where do we get it?" said Angel. She remembered that when she helped her mother with the pork chop gravy, flour got added to some juice. But where had that juice come from?

She opened the cupboard door and looked in.

"Ketchup is like gravy," said Rags. "Sort of."

"I don't know —" said Angel. "Maybe a little wouldn't hurt." She opened the ketchup and poured some into the pot. She stirred it with a spoon. It seemed to disappear.

"Put in more!" said Rags.

Angel poured some more into the pot. This

time it didn't disappear. It began to bubble.

"It looks good!" said Rags.

Angel had to admit it was beginning to look good. And it was beginning to smell! That was very important — that the dinner smell good in the house as it cooked.

"But it should be brown," said Angel. "It looks red. I never saw red gravy." She opened the cupboard again. Rags pointed to a box with a picture of gravy over mashed potatoes.

"Gravy mix!" said Angel. "Brown gravy mix, just what we need!" She tore open the box and stirred the brown powder into the pot. "It's too thick!" she shouted. "Get something to make it wetter, Rags, hurry!"

"Milk?" said Rags hopefully.

"No, something gravy colored. Dark."

Rags opened a can of Pepsi-Cola and poured it into the pot. Angel opened her mouth to object, but it was too late. It was already in the pot. And it looked right. It did look like gravy. Angel stirred it up and put the cover on.

"Now we just have to wait till it cooks into a

delicious dinner and the house smells like Margaret's."

Angel and Rags cleaned up the anchovy can and potato skins and washed the dishes in the sink. Then they got out the good dishes from the top shelf of the cupboard and the good silverware and napkins.

"We could put a candle on the table too," said Rags.

By the time all of this was done, they could smell the stew cooking. "Ummmm," said Rags, rubbing his stomach. "It smells good!"

Angel took off the cover and stirred the stew again. Then she put the spoon to her lips and tasted it. "It is good!" said Angel. "It just needs — a little something."

"A little something," echoed Rags. "What?"

"Spices," said Angel, going to the spice rack.

"How do we know which one?" said Rags.

Angel studied the bottles. "I think stew should have just a little of everything," she said.

Rags quickly opened every bottle and Angel

sprinkled a small amount of each into the pot. Then she stirred it and tasted it again. "That's better!" she said. "It's a little burny, like chili. But it's definitely stew," she added.

"Now we'll just rest and wait," she said. Angel sat down at the kitchen table. Rags sat beside her. "I think we definitely did something good," said Angel. "I am sure there is no way Mom could not notice. And no way she wouldn't be pleased that we made dinner for her. Is there?" she said.

"She'll like dinner," said Rags, obligingly. "What else are we having, Angel?"

"Else?" said Angel.

"For supper."

"Nothing else. That's the good thing about stew. It has everything in it. You don't need anything else."

"Anything-stew has anything in it, anything in it!" sang Rags.

Angel closed her eyes and savored her mother's surprise. ". . . and Angel and Rags did it all by themselves," she could hear her mother saying on the phone the next day. "Why, yes, they didn't use a mix or anything. They cooked a real stew!"

She'd probably even invite Alyce to stay for dinner, when she came in. Then Alyce would notice that not everything Angel did ended in disaster, or annoyance. Angel was capable of doing good things, grown-up things. Maybe her mother would be so proud she'd even invite other neighbors in . . .

Angel's dream was broken by the sound of a car at the curb.

"Mom's home!" said Rags, running outside to the car.

Angel ran to the window to see if her mother had noticed the smell yet. Her mother and Alyce were unloading the grocery bags from the car. As they started up the sidewalk, her mother called to her, "Angel? I got hamburgers at the drive-in for supper! Here, Rags, yours has every-thing on it, the way you like it."

Any other day, Angel would have been glad to see hamburgers. Not today. She watched Rags, the traitor, open up his hamburger and begin to eat it before he was even up the steps, singing "Everything-on-it, everything-on-it," a variation of his stew song. Her mother bustled in the door, saying, "Alyce and I tried this new restaurant where they have the best clam chowder..."

Angel couldn't believe her ears. This time she was sure she had done something good. She hadn't been able to see a single way anything could go wrong. Cooking supper for her mother was bound to be a good thing. Unless, of course, her mother had *eaten* supper and purchased hamburgers for the children. And of all insults, her mother had not noticed the wonderful smell coming from the kitchen. "Why don't I just face it?" thought Angel. "Nothing I ever do is right. I might just as well get used to always being wrong."

She watched Rags chewing happily away on his hamburger, forgetting about the stew they had made so lovingly only a short time ago. Angel sighed and began to carry groceries in with her mother.

Suddenly Mrs. O'Leary began to sniff the air. Angel's hopes began to rise slightly. Her mother frowned.

"Angel," she said. "Something is burning. You and Rags haven't been playing with matches, have you?"

Angel toyed with the idea of fleeing from the scene and throwing herself dramatically onto her bed. That would certainly make her mother notice her. Or she could jump out of a window and leave a note behind listing all the times she was misunderstood and all the things she tried to do that were good but went unnoticed. Here was her dinner simmering away in the kitchen and her mother asked her if she'd been playing with matches. While she was trying to decide about being dramatic, she heard Rags's voice.

"It's stew," he was saying. "Angel and I made it for dinner."

"Stew?" her mother was saying in an incredulous voice. "Why!"—she was lifting the cover—"so it is!"

"We made it ourselves," Rags was saying importantly.

"Yourselves!" their mother repeated.

"We made it for you for dinner."

"For dinner!"

Her mother sounded like a parrot.

"Angel?" called Mrs. O'Leary in the voice she used when they had company. Angel was deterred from action by her mother's call. "Come here, dear!"

"You've had supper," said Angel crossly. "And Rags is eating a hamburger. It's too late."

"Too late!" parroted her mother. "Of course it's not too late. Alyce and I just had a little bit of clam chowder and Rags can finish the hamburger later," she said, snatching it from Rags and putting it on top of the refrigerator, out of his reach.

"Alyce, the children have made dinner," she

said, as if it was the most natural thing in the world. "Won't you stay and have some ... stew with us?"

"Why, I'd like that!" said Alyce.

"Rags, just put the plates around and we'll have a fine dinner!"

Rags set the table and Angel lit the candle in the middle and dished up four steaming dishes of stew. Her mother put a plate of crackers on the table to go with the stew.

Rags finished his dish of stew very quickly and asked for more. Angel felt heartened. Her mother ate hers more slowly and thoughtfully and studied her fork carefully between bites, but she appeared to be enjoying the meal. Alyce didn't question the ingredients at all but said, "Why, Angel, I'll have to get your recipe for this delicious stew."

"It's anything-stew!" said Rags. "Just put anything in a pot and stir it up!"

Alyce looked surprised. "Well, I'd need a recipe though, so I'd get the right amounts."

"No amounts, we didn't have amounts, did we, Angel?" Rags looked quizzically up at her. Angel ignored him.

When Angel took the first bite of the stew herself, she was very surprised. She didn't like it. Not at all. But it seemed that she was the only one not eating. She wondered how everyone else could possibly say it was good, let alone ask for more.

"Now, what," said her mother, "do you suppose these small brown vegetables are?"

"Raisins," said Rags quickly. He was proud to be able to identify raisins, because so many foods looked just alike to him. But raisins he knew. He liked raisins, in stew or out of it.

"Raisins?" said Angel, in surprise. "I didn't put raisins in."

"I did!" said Rags. "Anything-stew can have anything in it, you said. There's lots of things we didn't put in. We could have put lots more things in it."

"I think it's just fine as it is," said their mother,

finishing the last morsel from her dish. "It doesn't need another thing, Rags. It has everything it needs. You chose exactly the right things. Angel, that was very good of you to cook dinner, dear."

Her mother looked pleased. Angel couldn't believe her eyes. Her mother *was* pleased. She liked the awful stew. Alyce and Rags liked the awful stew. She was the only one who didn't like it. Her mother had said the words she had wanted to hear and had noticed the good thing that Angel had tried to do, even when it had turned out awful.

Angel was puzzled. She had started out to do a good thing. Then it had turned into a bad thing. And now it was a good thing again! She decided to stop trying to figure things out. Acting grown-up and mature was a lot more complicated than she had expected.

EIGHT

Angel Smiles

Some of the awful anything-stew was left over and put into a bowl that was kept in the refrigerator. Even though Rags had it for lunch almost every day and Angel's mother had it for supper once again, there was always more stew in the bowl. It seemed to multiply like the loaves and fishes in the Bible story. Finally, one morning a week later, Angel noticed that it was gone, and she breathed a sigh of relief. She wouldn't do any more cooking for a while, she decided. Her mother's dinners tasted far better than hers.

Angel went out to sit on the back steps. Rags was digging under the porch. Their mother was cleaning closets and looking over Angel's school clothes. Angel watched the cars go by, as she did so many mornings. Suddenly, a long way down the block, she saw someone on a bicycle. The bicycle handlebars seemed to have a red flag attached to them, one that was blowing and waving as the bicycle moved.

Angel squinted. Then she saw that the girl riding the bike was Edna, who was in her room at school, and the flag that was waving was a red swimming suit. When the bike got in front of Angel's house, Angel waved.

"Edna?" she called. "What are you doing around here?" No one from Angel's school lived nearby, at least no one in her grade.

Edna dragged her feet and came to a stop.

"Caroline?" said Edna. "I didn't know you lived over here. I'm going to the pool to swim."

Angel was surprised to hear that someone her own age was going to the pool alone. She closed her eyes and tried to imagine what it would be like, riding a bike across town with her swimsuit flying on the handlebars, without Rags pulling at her shirt.

"Why don't you come?" said Edna, brushing her hair back from her eyes and resnapping it into a brown barrette.

Angel looked around to see who was there.

"Why don't you come?" Edna said again. She seemed to be talking to Angel. Did she realize what she was saying?

"Do you have a suit?"

Angel's mind was spinning now, and she had to work hard to focus on these new words of Edna's. A suit. A swimming suit, she must mean. Angel thought of the swimming suit with the little ruffled skirt that she had had since she was seven. "It stretches," her mother said, "and you only wear it in the yard under the sprinkler."

Angel shook her head. "It's too small," she said, relieved that she didn't have to think up an excuse, or maybe even tell a lie.

"You can go in your shorts," said Edna, sweeping all of Angel's relief out of the way in seconds. "C'mon."

This girl has no idea what she is saying, thought Angel. C'mon. Just as though all she, Angel, had to do was get up and walk out of the yard without a thought in the world about her Responsibility. About Rags and his life that she almost failed with once. She would never desert him again.

"I have to watch my brother," said Angel. Edna looked around for a brother.

"He's under the porch," said Angel. "Aren't you, Rags?" called Angel, in case Edna should think she was making her brother up. Rags pounded on the porch floor with his shovel. Then he stuck his head out of the latticework, like a troll under a bridge.

"Isn't your mom home?" said Edna.

Angel sighed. It wasn't easy to explain her mother to strangers who evidently lived very different lives from hers, she decided. They

apparently didn't know the dangers of living —
speeding cars, high places, falling objects. Life
was fraught with danger. She wondered how
Edna lived to be ten. And who took care of her
small brothers and sisters?

"My mom is home," began Angel, "but —"

"Go ask," said Edna, leaning her bike on the
fence and sitting down on the steps to wait.
Edna didn't waste words. "And then you can
come over to my house and play Monopoly or
something after."

Angel couldn't believe her ears. Just like it was
all settled. Just like she did this every day of her
life! Angel had never been to anyone's house to
play Monopoly. Even during the school year she
had to come right home after school so that her
mother would know nothing had happened to
her and she was safe. And, of course, Rags was
always waiting for her, his face pressed against
the cold window all winter long, waiting for
three o'clock.

"Have you got a bike?" said Edna, interrupt-
ing Angel's reverie.

Angel shook her head. It was dangerous to ride bikes in the street and there was a law that said you couldn't ride on the sidewalk, which would be the safe place to ride. Mrs. O'Leary had known someone whose daughter was riding a bike when it hit a rock and she was thrown over the handlebars to the pavement and was in the hospital for six months with a concussion. Angel's old tricycle was in the garage. She wouldn't be seen on that anymore. Rags rode it now and then, but Angel never did. Not since she was five.

"I'll ride slow," said Edna. "Go and ask," she said, motioning her head toward the house anxiously.

Angel stood up. Of course. Why not ask? Her mother would say "No, of course not," and then it would be all over, this impossible otherlife that had come her way today. She needn't think of excuses. Her mother would say no, and that was that. Nobody could argue with her mother.

"OK," said Angel. "I'll be right back."

Edna traced the floorboards on the porch with the key to her bicycle lock and began to hum. Angel ran up the stairs two at a time. Her mother had her head in Angel's closet, among the winter coats and jackets.

"What is it, dear?" she asked in a muffled voice.

"Can I go swimming at the pool with Edna, and over to her house to play, afterward?" Angel said, all in one breath without stopping. She sat down on the bed and waited for her mother to mention Rags and safety.

Her mother's head detached itself from the hanging clothes. Her hair stood on end. "Edna?" she said.

"She's a girl in my room at school."

Her mother pursed her lips the way she did when Danger threatened one of her children. "Yes," said her mother firmly. "I think it would be a good idea for you to go swimming with Edna."

Angel felt the bed sway under her. Her mother must have heard her incorrectly.

"I've been thinking about it lately, Angel, and

you need to have friends. I mean it's not *healthy* for you to be around Rags and me all the time. You are ten years old and you need more freedom." Her mother patted her on the head. "You go with Edna and have a good time. And go to her house afterward. Just write down her address and phone number so I know where you are."

Her mother's head was back in the closet now, giving muffled warnings to look both ways at the corners and call home when she got to Edna's house and for heaven's sake don't go into deep water.

Angel stood up and started down the steps slowly. She felt as though she had lost several pounds, that if she put out her arms she would rise from the ground and fly away. Over her house, over the pool, away, away. Today it was the pool and Monopoly. Who knew what would come tomorrow?

Perhaps Edna would suggest she stay for supper, and even overnight! They would lie in bed and tell each other secrets the way real friends did in books, and share candy bars and exchange records and maybe even clothes. She would come home and tell Rags about what they did at Edna's house and how they lived and about the swimming pool and how she learned the jellyfish float. Everyone would say, "Who is that girl?" and they'd think she must be a friend of Edna's, and pretty soon they would all wave and say, "Hi Caroline," and just expect to see her coming and going. Maybe there would be other people from St. Mary's and they could all go to the drugstore for ice cream together and push and shove each other around, laughing, like the big kids did that Angel saw when she went there with her mother to get a prescription filled.

Angel opened the back door and walked out on to the back porch. "I can go," she said to Edna.

"Good," said Edna, putting up the kickstand on her bike.

Angel lifted the latticework on the porch to say good-bye to Rags. He came out and pressed his face on the fence. He looked like he might cry, but it was probably just the dirt on his face.

"Who's going to take care of me?" he asked.

"You are," said Angel, giving him a hug. "Mom's upstairs, and I'll be home soon."

"Caroline?" said Edna. "You need a towel and some shorts."

"I'll get them," said Angel. And then, although Alyce was not there to notice, Angel smiled.